D0473916

SPONGEBOB GOES GREEN!

AN EARTH-FRIENDLY ADVENTURE

by Molly Reisner   illustrated by Stephen Reed

SIMON SPOTLIGHT/NICKELODEON
New York   London   Toronto   Sydney

Stephen Hillenburg (signature)

Based on the TV series *SpongeBob SquarePants*® created by Stephen Hillenburg as seen on Nickelodeon®

SIMON SPOTLIGHT

An imprint of Simon & Schuster Children's Publishing Division

1230 Avenue of the Americas, New York, New York 10020

Manufactured in the United States of America

10 9 8 7

ISBN-13: 978-1-4169-4985-5

ISBN-10: 1-4169-4985-2

0210 LAK

It was a chilly spring morning in Bikini Bottom. SpongeBob ████ to get to work on time when he bumped into Sandy.

"Hey, SpongeBob! Want to go hang gliding off Seaweed Cliff with me?" she asked. "It's the first sunny day of the year and I sure as sugar don't want to miss it!"

"No can do, Sandy," replied SpongeBob. "Mr. Krabs has a surprise for me! I have to get to work!"

"You again?" Squidward grumbled as SpongeBob bounded through the Krusty Krab doors.

Just then Mr. Krabs burst into the dining room.

"Fry Cook SpongeBob reporting for duty and surprises, sir!" said SpongeBob, turning to face Mr. Krabs.

"Ahoy, crew!" Mr. Krabs replied excitedly, waving a claw in the air. "Follow me, boys!"

Mr. Krabs led them outside and showed off the brand-new pool behind the Krusty Krab!

"A private pool for your hard-working staff?" Squidward inquired hopefully.

"Welcome to the Krusty Krab Pool, FOR PAYING CUSTOMERS ONLY!" Mr. Krabs replied. "The grand opening is tomorrow. SpongeBob, I need you to be the pool manager."

"MANAGER!? It's an honor, sir!" cried SpongeBob happily.

The next day Mr. Krabs gathered his customers outside for an announcement.
"In honor of our pool opening, I hereby offer a penny off admission!"
Then SpongeBob cut the ceremonial ribbon. "Don't rush in all at once!"
reminded SpongeBob. "And wait an hour after you eat to enter the pool!"
But no one seemed excited. No one was even lined up to get in!

"It's too cold to swim," whined a little girl. "Spring just started!"

"Yeah!" mumbled the crowd, walking back inside to finish their meals.

"I'm already losing money on me money-making scheme!" fretted Mr. Krabs.

"Hmmm. Maybe we can have another reopening in summer?" offered SpongeBob.

Mr. Krabs gazed sadly into the glistening, empty pool. Suddenly an idea popped into his head. "Or maybe we'll just make summer come early this year!"

The following morning SpongeBob was on his way to work when he noticed a big, black cloud of smoke puffing out from the roof of the Krusty Krab.

"Oh, no!" cried SpongeBob, racing off toward the restaurant. "I'll save you, Mr. Krabs!"

SpongeBob found Mr. Krabs standing next to a chugging boat. He was pumping the exhaust from the boat through the roof and into the air outside.

"Hey, I didn't know you had inside parking!" exclaimed SpongeBob.

Mr. Krabs chuckled. "I'm just pumpin' a wee bit of carbon dioxide into the air. It'll warm up the temperature and bring on an endless summer! People will want to use me new pool all year long!" he explained.

"Ooh!" cried SpongeBob excitedly. "The endless summer does sound fun, AND profitable! I just wish it could be the endless summer right now."

Later that day SpongeBob brought Patrick to the boatyard. "I've got a plan with your name on it!" said SpongeBob.

Patrick scratched his head. "Your plan's name is Patrick?"

"Nope! The plan is called: We Need to Borrow These Boats So We Can Release More Carbon Dioxide into the Air to Help Mr. Krabs Speed Up Summer and Open His Pool Sooner So I Can Be Pool Manager!" SpongeBob said breathlessly.

Patrick snapped his fingers. "Gotcha! Wait, what's carbon dioxide again?" he asked.

SpongeBob thought for a moment. "Hmm, I'm not really sure. But more of it in the atmosphere makes it warmer, according to Mr. Krabs, which will help us bring on the endless summer!" declared SpongeBob.

SpongeBob and Patrick lugged several boats inside the Krusty Krab and began pumping carbon dioxide into the atmosphere, just like Mr. Krabs had done.

Next they gathered a whole bunch of tires and started burning them. More smoke floated up into the sky.

"Soon it'll be so hot, the pool will be filled with people," SpongeBob said happily. "Then I'll get to start my new job as pool manager!"

To pump more carbon dioxide into the atmosphere, they wasted electricity by turning on lots of lights and appliances.

"Wow, look at all that carbon stuff," Patrick said. "Is summer supposed to smell this smoky?"

"I'm sure it's harmless, Patrick," SpongeBob answered. "Otherwise Mr. Krabs wouldn't have said it was okay!"

Soon it warmed up and people came to the pool. SpongeBob was so excited to start pool manager duty, but his excitement faded when Sandy arrived.

"What are you doing messin' with Mother Nature?" she cried out angrily. "You're pollutin' Bikini Bottom with all this carbon dioxide and bringin' on global warming!"

"What's global warming?" SpongeBob asked.

"Have you been under a rock or something?" Sandy replied, shocked.

"No, but Patrick has."

"Never mind. Ya see, Earth has these gases called greenhouse gases. They're in the atmosphere to keep the temperature of the planet just right. Carbon dioxide is one of these gases. But when we make more greenhouse gases than the planet needs naturally, like you've been doin' by burnin' tires and fuel, it locks the heat in the atmosphere. That makes the planet hotter than it should be. That's global warming. And that's not good."

"It's not? But that's exactly what we want," SpongeBob interrupted. "Right, Mr. Krabs?"

Mr. Krabs scooted away as quickly as his feet could carry him.

Sandy just shook her head. "No, SpongeBob! When that happens, it's hard for plants to grow and our seasons get real messed up. And I for one refuse to come to the Krusty Krab until you stop all your pollutin' and damagin' our environment!"

That night SpongeBob thought about what Sandy had said about global warming. He began to feel bad about what he had done. "Is adding a little carbon dioxide into the air really hurting where we live?" he asked Gary.

Gary slithered inside his shell. "I didn't think so either, ol' Gar-Bear. Sandy is probably just overreacting," SpongeBob told himself.

But the temperature in Bikini Bottom continued to rise. SpongeBob tried to focus on the silver lining—his job as pool manager was so much fun!

But soon the weather became unbearably hot and the pool was overcrowded. People were pushing and shoving one another from all sides just trying to get a leg or arm in the pool to cool off! SpongeBob was blowing his whistle left and right trying to keep order.

"I love the customers, but this heat is frying my shell!" cried Mr. Krabs.

The next day the water in the pool
started sizzling. Then the level of the water
began sinking really fast!

"Mr. Krabs!" SpongeBob cried out. "What's
happening to the water?"

"It's evaporating because of the heat!" Mr. Krabs answered.
The customers were hot, cranky, and angry that they had paid
money to go swimming in a pool that now had no water! SpongeBob
tried to refill the pool, but the second the water hit the concrete it
evaporated.

"I think Sandy might be right about global warming after all," SpongeBob
said to himself.

SpongeBob rushed to Sandy's treedome to apologize, but no one was home. Next he went to find Patrick, but he was gone too. Even Squidward was nowhere to be found. All of his friends had disappeared! When he got home, he found a note from Gary.

"'Too hot here. Left for Murky Waters,'" SpongeBob read aloud.

"Oh, no. What have I done?" he cried.

SpongeBob and Mr. Krabs traveled to Murky Waters to apologize and convince everyone to come back home.

"All former Bikini Bottom residents," Mr. Krabs announced through a megaphone. "SpongeBob's really sorry he brought about global warming in Bikini Bottom! We wanted an endless summer, but we didn't realize how much damage it would cause."

Soon a crowd of familiar faces gathered outside.

"Why should we listen to you? You ruined our home!" a man grumbled. SpongeBob hung his head in shame. He grabbed the megaphone. "You're right. We did. And my good friend Sandy tried to warn us and we didn't listen. But now we want to fix our mistakes. Maybe if we all work together, we can restore Bikini Bottom to what it used to be!"

SpongeBob could see Sandy poking her head out from the crowd. She started clapping and cheering. "SpongeBob is right! Let's go home, people!"

The residents of Bikini Bottom returned home and worked hard to make their community beautiful again. They planted trees to add oxygen back into the air. Instead of driving their motorized boats, which burn fuel for power, people started riding their bicycles more. To conserve energy, they used less electricity and unplugged appliances when they weren't being used. SpongeBob worked night and day to help repair the damage he created.

"You messed up big time," Sandy said one day when they were planting trees. "But I'm proud of everything you're doin' now, little fella!"

SpongeBob beamed. "Thanks, Sandy. I sure learned my lesson. I'll never forget how important our environment is again. Hey, want to go for a bike ride when we're done?"

Sandy thought for a moment. "Yeah, I know the perfect place for us to go!"

Sandy and SpongeBob biked to the Krusty Krab. There was a huge banner hanging up announcing a discount on admission to the Krusty Krab pool for any customer who walked or biked to the restaurant!

"It's the least I could do," said Mr. Krabs. Then he tossed SpongeBob his whistle and clipboard. "I still need a pool manager for the summer season, lad. And this time it's really summer."

Sandy and SpongeBob laughed. "Hooray for summer!" they yelled.